Nadeera Goonetilleke

Heartstrings

Heartstrings

Nadeera Goonetilleke

Published by Nadeera Goonetilleke, 2024.

HEARTSTRINGS

First edition. October 17, 2024.

ISBN: 979-8227037664

Written by Nadeera Goonetilleke.

Chapter 1: The Charming Days of Childhood

Arun and his sister Neha grew up in a small, picturesque village called, Willow Brook where time seemed to move slower, savoring every moment. Their days were filled with simple joys: climbing trees, chasing each other through sun-soaked fields, and playing with Meera, the adorable little girl who lived next door. Meera, with her bright eyes and infectious laugh, was younger by several years, but that didn't stop Arun and Neha from treating her as their own little sister.

One afternoon, as the three of them gathered under the shade of a sprawling banyan tree, Meera came running towards them, her tiny feet barely touching the ground.

"Look! I found the prettiest flowers!" Meera exclaimed, her voice high-pitched with excitement as she held out a bundle of wildflowers.

Neha's eyes lit up. "Oh, Meera, you always find the best ones! Come here, let me hold you."

"No way!" Arun interrupted, reaching out to scoop Meera into his arms. "It's my turn to carry her!"

Neha laughed and tugged at Meera's other hand. "No, it's not! I didn't get my turn yet today!"

Meera, caught in the middle of their playful tug-of-war, giggled uncontrollably. "Both of you carry me!" she squealed, her laughter echoing through the fields.

Arun rolled his eyes, finally letting Neha take her. "Alright, fine. But tomorrow, she's mine!"

With Meera perched securely on Neha's back, they wandered down the path toward the village stream, the warmth of their bond palpable in the air. Arun couldn't help but smile as Meera's laughter filled the afternoon. She was like a little bundle of sunshine that lit up their world in the most unexpected ways.

But it wasn't just playfulness that bound the three of them. Meera had a special way of turning ordinary moments into magical ones. She would insist on helping with their chores, even though her small hands could barely hold the broom, and she would pester them to join her in dancing to the old folk songs that played on the village radio. Arun and Neha adored her, fiercely protective of her innocence.

Yet, their days of carefree laughter came to an abrupt halt when Arun and Neha's father got transferred to a distant city. That evening, as the news settled in, the house felt eerily quiet. Arun looked at Neha, who was sitting on their porch, staring at the setting sun.

"Neha, we'll come back to visit," Arun said softly, trying to comfort her—and perhaps, himself too.

"But what about Meera?" Neha whispered, her voice barely audible. "Who's going to play with her when we're gone?"

Arun sighed, not having an answer to that. "I guess she'll have to make new friends."

Chapter 2: A Sudden Departure

The day their father announced his transfer to the bustling city, the world seemed to shift. The once peaceful life Arun and Neha had known in the village now felt fragile, as if it was slipping through their fingers. Their hearts weighed heavy, especially when they thought about leaving Meera behind. How would they explain to her that their simple, joyful days together were ending?

The morning of their departure was filled with an unnatural stillness. Arun and Neha hadn't spoken much; there was nothing left to say that could ease the sadness in their hearts. Their father was already busy packing the last of their belongings, while their mother tried to mask her sorrow with a forced smile. They all knew what had to be done, but it didn't make the leaving any easier.

"Are we really going to leave her like this?" Neha whispered to Arun as they stood outside Meera's house, hesitating.

Arun sighed deeply, his chest tightening. "We don't have a choice."

Neha blinked back tears and nodded, trying to be strong. "Let's just go inside."

When they entered Meera's home, the little girl came bounding towards them, her bright eyes sparkling with joy, unaware of the gravity of what was about to happen.

"Are you going on a trip?" Meera asked innocently, clutching her favorite doll tightly to her chest.

Arun's throat tightened as he knelt down to her level. He didn't know how to tell her. How could he make her understand that they wouldn't be back for a long time, maybe not even for years? He ruffled her soft hair gently, trying to hold back his own emotions.

"Yeah, we're going away for a bit, Meera. But..." His voice cracked, and he forced a smile. "You'll be just fine, champ. You've got your mom and dad here. You're going to be okay."

Meera's smile faltered, and her little brow furrowed in confusion. "But when will you come back?"

Neha, unable to hold back any longer, knelt beside her brother, her voice trembling as she tried to explain. "We'll come back as soon as we can, sweetie. I promise."

Meera's bottom lip quivered, and her small hand reached out to hold onto Neha's dress, as if she could somehow keep them from leaving. "Can't I come with you?" she asked, her voice so small, so filled with hope, it nearly broke Neha's heart.

Before Neha could respond, Meera's mother, standing quietly in the doorway, stepped forward and crouched down beside them. She gently stroked Meera's hair, trying to soothe her. "They have to go, darling. But don't worry, when they come back, they'll bring you sweets. Won't you, Arun? Neha?"

Both siblings nodded, though the promise of sweets felt like a weak consolation for the loss Meera was about to feel. Meera's big, innocent eyes filled with tears, and she clung to Neha, burying her face in her shoulder.

"I don't want you to go," Meera whispered, her little body shaking with sobs.

Arun closed his eyes, his heart aching with every tear she shed. He had never felt so helpless. He wished there was something he could say, some magic words that would take away her pain. But there were none.

Neha held Meera tightly, whispering soothing words, though her own tears betrayed her. "We don't want to go either, sweetie. But we'll think of you every day, ok."

Meera sniffled, her tiny hands gripping Neha's dress as if letting go would mean losing them forever. "You promise?"

Arun swallowed hard and knelt down next to them. He took Meera's hand in his, his voice thick with emotion. "We promise, Meera. We'll never forget you."

Meera's tears slowed, but she looked up at them, her face streaked with sadness.

Meera's mother gave them a gentle nod, silently telling them it was time to go. Arun and Neha stood slowly, their hearts heavy with the weight of leaving behind their dear little friend.

As they turned to leave, Meera's tiny voice called out one last time. "You'll come back, right?"

Both siblings stopped in their tracks, turning back to look at her, their eyes filled with unspoken emotions.

"We will, Meera," Arun said, his voice almost breaking. "We will."

With one final glance, they walked out of Meera's house, the sound of her soft sobs following them as they made their way home. Neither of them spoke as they packed up the last of their belongings, their hearts too full of sorrow to find any words.

Later that afternoon, as the car pulled away from the village, Arun and Neha looked back through the rear window. Meera stood by the doorway of her house, waving with all her might, her small figure growing smaller and smaller until she disappeared from view.

And just like that, their childhood came to an end.

Chapter 3: Life in the City

The move to the city had shaken their world, but after a few weeks, Arun and Neha found themselves slowly adjusting to their new surroundings. The city was a whirlwind of activity—towering buildings, crowded streets, honking cars, and an endless stream of faces, each caught up in their own hurried lives. It was nothing like the peaceful, open skies of the village, Willow brook they had left behind.

In the beginning, Arun and Neha couldn't stop talking about Meera. The memories of her small hands grasping theirs, her innocent laughter, and her wide, curious eyes followed them everywhere.

"Do you remember how Meera would get so excited about the smallest things?" Neha asked one evening, a soft smile playing on her lips. They were sitting in the living room, both trying to do their homework but distracted by memories.

Arun nodded, looking up from his textbooks, his eyes softening. "Yeah. She used to think the stars in the sky were fireflies. She'd ask me to catch them for her."

Neha laughed, though there was a sadness behind her laughter. "And you always tried, just to make her happy."

They fell into silence, each lost in their own thoughts of the little girl they had left behind. The ache of missing her was still fresh, but they had to focus on the present. The demands of their new school and the pressure to fit in quickly filled their days.

As the weeks turned into months, their conversations about Meera grew less frequent. Arun's schoolwork intensified, and soon he was occupied with extracurricular activities, making new friends, and navigating the complexities of city life. Neha too found herself buried in her own academic pursuits. With each passing day, the memories of their village life, and of Meera, began to fade into the background.

One evening, during dinner a few years later, their father introduced a topic that would become a pivotal moment in Arun's life.

"You know, Arun," their father said, his voice calm but firm as usual, "there's a lot of potential for you in the police force. You've got the discipline, and you're sharp. You should think about following in my footsteps."

Arun looked up, surprised by the suggestion. He hadn't given much thought to what he wanted to do with his life yet. The idea of becoming a police officer had never crossed his mind, but there was something about the way his father said it—so sure, so certain—that made him pause.

"I don't know, Dad," Arun replied, setting down his fork. "I was thinking about business or something."

Their father raised an eyebrow, his serious gaze fixed on Arun. "Business? You think the corporate world is going to give you the same sense of purpose that serving your country will?"

Neha watched the exchange closely, her usual quiet self when her father spoke, but her eyes darted between them, sensing the importance of the conversation.

"I just don't know if it's for me," Arun said, hesitating.

Their father leaned back in his chair, crossing his arms. "Give it some thought. There's no rush. But trust me, Arun, the path of a police officer is challenging, yes, but it's rewarding in ways you can't even imagine."

After that night, Arun couldn't shake the idea. Slowly, the thought of joining the police force began to settle in his mind. The more he thought about it, the more it appealed to him. By the time he finished college, he had made up his mind—he would follow in his father's footsteps.

Meanwhile, Neha found her calling in teaching. She loved the idea of shaping young minds, of being the kind of teacher who made a difference in her students' lives. She was gentle, patient, and empathetic—everything a good teacher should be. Their parents were proud of both of them, seeing how their children had grown into responsible, successful adults.

One evening, years after they had moved to the city, their father came home with an announcement.

"There's going to be a family gathering," he said, sitting down at the dinner table. "Your uncle is throwing a party. Everyone's invited, and I expect both of you to be there."

Arun exchanged a glance with Neha, neither of them particularly enthusiastic about the idea. Family gatherings were usually filled with relatives they barely knew, making small talk that often felt forced. But they both knew better than to argue.

"When is it?" Arun asked, his tone neutral.

"This weekend," their father replied, cutting into his food. "I don't want to hear any excuses about being too busy. It's important for us to show up."

Neha sighed softly, but nodded. "We'll be there, Dad."

Arun shrugged, pushing his plate away. "Yeah, we'll come."

Their father gave them a satisfied nod. "Good. It'll be nice to catch up with family."

As the weekend approached, Arun and Neha found themselves mentally preparing for the event. It wasn't that they didn't care about their relatives, but life in the city had made them distant from those ties. Still, they respected their father's wishes and knew that showing up was non-negotiable.

The day of the party arrived, and as they got dressed, Neha couldn't help but feel a sense of nostalgia creeping in.

"Do you remember the last time we went to one of these family gatherings?" she asked, glancing at Arun as she adjusted her earrings.

Arun smiled faintly, slipping on his jacket. "Yeah, back when we were kids. We used to run around with the other children, causing trouble."

Neha laughed. "I wonder if it'll feel the same."

Arun shook his head. "Probably not. But hey, at least we're doing this for Dad."

As they left the house and made their way to the party, neither of them could have predicted how this family gathering would lead to unexpected encounters and stir long-buried memories.

Chapter 4: An Unforgettable Night

As Arun and his family stepped into the grand house, they were immediately struck by its opulence. The chandeliers sparkled overhead, casting a warm glow across the vast room that was already filled with the buzz of conversation and laughter. The party had an air of sophistication, far more elegant than Arun had expected. A popular band played lively music in the corner, setting the perfect mood for the evening.

"This is... something," Arun muttered to Neha as they glanced around, taking in the grand decor and the crowd of well-dressed guests mingling across the room.

Neha grinned. "Looks like Uncle went all out for this one. I'm impressed."

Their father gave a slight nod of approval. "He's always been the one to enjoy big gatherings. Now, don't just stand around—go mingle. Meet your cousins. And don't forget, be on your best behavior," he added with a stern but affectionate look.

As they moved further into the room, they were greeted by relatives, some familiar and others whose names they struggled to remember. Arun and Neha were soon swept into conversations with cousins their age. Arun exchanged handshakes, nods, and friendly smiles, feeling surprisingly relaxed. The formal atmosphere quickly gave way to casual chatter, with laughter echoing around the space as they enjoyed drinks and snacks served by well-dressed waiters.

A little while later, the band shifted gears, playing a slower tune, and couples began to fill the dance floor. Arun, standing with a glass of Coke, glanced around the room. That's when he noticed her—across the crowd, standing with a group of friends, was a girl who immediately caught his attention. She had a lively presence, laughing with those around her, her confidence and charm radiating from her every movement. Her long, flowing dress shimmered under the light, and her eyes sparkled as she glanced in his direction, offering a soft smile.

Arun felt a strange flutter in his chest, something he hadn't felt before. "Who's that?" he whispered to Neha, who was standing beside him.

Neha followed his gaze and grinned. "Looks like someone's caught your eye. Why don't you go find out?"

I don't know... She seems way out of my league," Arun confessed, feeling his nerves begin to rise.

"Oh, come on, Arun. You're a handsome guy. Just go say hi. What's the worst that could happen?" Neha nudged him playfully.

With a deep breath, Arun gathered his courage and walked toward the girl. His heart raced, but he tried to appear calm as he approached her. She turned her head just as he neared, her eyes meeting his again, and this time her smile widened, playful and inviting.

"Hi," Arun began, feeling a bit awkward but pushing through it. "I'm Arun. I was wondering if you'd like to dance."

The girl's smile deepened, and she looked him up and down with amused curiosity. "I thought you'd never ask," she replied, her voice soft but confident.

They moved onto the dance floor as the music played a soft, romantic melody. Arun's hand rested on her waist, while she placed her hand gently in his. As they began to sway to the music, Arun couldn't help but notice how effortlessly they moved together, as if they had danced many times before.

"I'm Riya, by the way," she said, her eyes twinkling as she glanced up at him. "Are you one of Uncle's nephews?"

"Yeah, I am," Arun replied with a slight chuckle. "My dad's his younger brother. I don't think we've met before."

Riya smiled and replied, "I don't think so. I don't often come to these gatherings; I'm just a friend of your uncle's daughter. But it's great to meet you! By the way, you dance beautifully!"

Arun felt a surge of confidence at her compliment. "Thanks. You're pretty great yourself. I didn't expect to be dancing tonight."

"Well, I'm glad you did," Riya said with a flirtatious smile. "It's been a while since I've had this much fun at one of these family events."

As the song continued, they danced in sync, their conversation flowing naturally. Arun couldn't help but be captivated by her charm. She was easy to talk to, and her laughter was infectious. They exchanged stories about their lives in the city, their experiences growing up, and even a few shared jokes about their eccentric relatives. The more they talked, the more Arun felt drawn to her. Riya wasn't just beautiful; she was witty, confident, and full of life.

As the evening progressed, the band announced a special dancing competition, encouraging couples to join in. Riya's eyes lit up with excitement.

"Come on, Arun, let's enter!" she said, tugging on his hand.

"Are you sure?" Arun asked, surprised by her enthusiasm.

"Of course! What's the point of a party if you don't have a little fun?"

Arun laughed, feeling a rush of energy from her boldness. "Alright, let's do it."

The competition began, and as they twirled and spun across the dance floor, Arun felt completely at ease with Riya. Her laughter rang out as they moved, her joy contagious. They danced through several rounds, their connection growing stronger with every step. By the final round, they were one of the last couples remaining, and with a flourish of applause, the judges declared them the winners.

"We did it!" Riya exclaimed, beaming up at Arun as they caught their breath.

Arun grinned, still a bit in disbelief. "Yeah, I can't believe it. You're pretty amazing."

"You're not so bad yourself," Riya teased, her smile softening as she looked at him. "I had a great time tonight."

"Me too," Arun replied, his voice a little quieter now, feeling the weight of the moment. As the party began to wind down, Arun realized that the night had been more special than he could have ever imagined. He didn't want it to end.

Before they parted ways, Arun hesitated for a moment, then spoke. "Hey, can I... get your number? I'd really like to stay in touch."

Riya's smile turned into a knowing grin as she handed him her phone. "I was wondering when you'd ask."

They exchanged numbers, and as Arun saved her contact, his heart raced with a mixture of excitement and nervousness. "I'll call you soon," he promised, feeling something he hadn't felt before—a genuine connection.

"I'll be waiting," Riya replied with a playful wink before disappearing into the crowd.

As Arun left the party with his family, his mind was filled with thoughts of Riya. He had never expected that a family gathering, something he had dreaded, would lead to his first real connection with someone like her. It felt like the beginning of something special, and for the first time in a long while, Arun was excited to see where it might lead.

Chapter 5: Midnight Conversations

The ride home after the party was calm and content. Arun's parents chatted about family matters, while Neha rested against the window, half-asleep. But Arun's mind was elsewhere—lost in thoughts of Riya. He replayed the moments they had shared, her laugh, the graceful way she danced, and the warmth in her eyes when they said goodbye.

As they pulled up to their home, his mother turned in her seat to look at them. "You two seemed to enjoy yourselves tonight," she said with a smile.

Neha stirred and yawned. "Yeah, it wasn't as boring as I thought it would be," she mumbled.

Arun chuckled. "Speak for yourself. I had a great time."

His father glanced at him in the rearview mirror, his tone curious. "You were dancing with someone, weren't you?"

Arun tried to play it cool, shrugging. "Yeah, just one of the guests. We got along pretty well."

Neha raised an eyebrow, suddenly more alert. "Oh really? And what's her name?"

"Riya," Arun replied, trying to keep his voice casual, though he could feel his face heat up.

His mother's eyes sparkled with interest. "She seemed like a nice girl. Very well-mannered."

"Mom, you barely saw her for two minutes," Arun laughed.

"But a mother can tell," she said with a knowing smile. "You seemed happy around her."

Arun could only nod, realizing that his mother wasn't wrong. He had felt genuinely happy around Riya—happier than he had in a long time.

"Well, it's good to see you making new friends," his father added as they all stepped out of the car. "Just don't let it distract you from your responsibilities."

"Of course not, Dad," Arun replied, though his mind was already far from any responsibilities for the night. He glanced at his phone as they entered the house, hoping to see a message from Riya, but the screen remained blank.

After a quick shower, he threw himself onto his bed, staring up at the ceiling. The house was quiet, the night air cool as it drifted in through his window. His thoughts kept drifting back to Riya—the way her smile had lingered as they said goodbye, the feel of her hand in his as they danced. Before he could stop himself, he grabbed his phone and opened her contact.

Should I text her? He wondered, his thumb hovering over the screen. After a moment of hesitation, he took a deep breath and typed, "Hey, Riya. Hope you got home safe. I had a great time tonight."

He hit send and stared at the screen, waiting anxiously. A minute passed. Then two. And just as he started to think he might've been too eager, his phone buzzed with a reply.

"I had a great time too, Arun. You made the party a lot more fun than I expected."

Arun grinned, the excitement bubbling up inside him. *Maybe I'll call her*, he thought, his heart racing a little at the idea. Without overthinking it, he hit the call button.

Riya picked up after just a couple of rings. "Hey," she greeted, her voice soft and warm on the other end. "Calling already? You must've really missed me."

Arun laughed, feeling a little more at ease. "What can I say? It's not every day I meet someone who beats me in a dance competition."

Riya's laughter was light and infectious. "Oh, please. We both know you were the better dancer. I just made you look good."

Their conversation flowed naturally, starting with light teasing and memories of the party. Arun found himself getting more comfortable as the minutes turned into hours. He told her about his family, his job as a police officer, and how his father's strict nature had shaped him. In turn,

Riya shared her own stories—her love for painting, her close relationship with her older sister, and her own experiences of living in the city.

"What do you miss most about your childhood?" she asked at one point, her tone a little more thoughtful.

Arun paused, considering her question. "I think... the simplicity of it all. You know, life was just about playing, school, and not worrying about anything else. We didn't have the pressures of life breathing down our necks back then."

Riya sighed softly. "Yeah, I get that. Everything felt lighter, more carefree. Sometimes I wish we could go back to those days, even if just for a little while."

They grew more comfortable as they talked, the night deepening around them. Before long, the clock ticked past midnight, but neither of them seemed to notice.

"What about you?" Arun asked after a while. "Do you ever think about what kind of future you want?"

There was a brief pause on Riya's end before she answered. "I think about it a lot, actually. I want something meaningful, you know? Not just a career, but someone to share it all with. I guess... I'm looking for someone who understands me, who sees the world the way I do."

Arun smiled, feeling a tug at his heart. "I think you'll find that person, Riya. You seem like someone who knows exactly what you want."

"I hope so," she replied softly. "But enough about me. What about you, Arun? What kind of future do you want?"

He hesitated, his thoughts suddenly more serious. "I don't know. I used to think I had it all figured out—becoming a good police officer, making my family proud. But lately, I've realized that maybe there's more to life than just a job. Maybe it's about finding someone who makes everything feel right. Someone you can talk to for hours and still feel like there's so much more to say."

Riya's voice softened. "That sounds perfect."

As the hours slipped by, neither of them seemed to care that it was getting late. The conversation moved from light-hearted stories to deeper thoughts about life, love, and dreams. Arun found himself opening up to Riya in a way he hadn't with anyone else before. It felt easy—natural.

At one point, Arun glanced at the clock and realized with a start that it was nearly 3 a.m. "Wow," he said, his voice filled with surprise. "I didn't realize we've been talking for four hours."

Riya giggled. "I guess time flies when you're having fun."

"Yeah... I really enjoyed this," Arun admitted, his voice quieter now. "It feels like I've known you forever."

"Same here," Riya replied, her tone just as soft. "I didn't expect to have such a great conversation tonight. I'm really glad you called."

Arun felt warmth spread through him at her words. "I'll call again soon. If that's okay?"

"I'd like that," Riya said, her voice full of sincerity.

As they said their goodnights, Arun hung up, feeling an unfamiliar sense of contentment. He lay back on his bed, staring up at the ceiling, a smile lingering on his face. This wasn't just any girl—Riya was different. There was something about her that made him believe she could be more than just a passing connection. She might just be the person he had been waiting for all along.

Chapter 6: A Painful Realization

The last few months had been a whirlwind for Arun. His career as a police officer, following in his father's footsteps, had consumed most of his time. He barely had a moment to himself, let alone time to spend with Riya. Their late-night phone calls had become fewer, and even when they did speak, it often felt rushed. But Riya had always been patient, understanding that his work was important and that he was building his future.

Arun had confidence in her, sure that their relationship was strong enough to withstand the distance and the demands of his job. He often found himself thinking about the next time he could see her—planning moments in his mind, imagining her smile when they would finally meet again. His father's constant reminders to stay focused and dedicated to his career echoed in his mind, but he kept telling himself that there would be time for love later.

But life, as he was about to learn, had a cruel way of surprising people.

One late afternoon, on his way to the police station, Arun found himself stuck in a massive traffic jam. The honking of cars and the slow crawl of vehicles did little to ease his growing frustration. He glanced out the window, his mind preoccupied with the day's duties, when something—or rather, someone—caught his eye.

It was Riya.

At first, he felt a surge of happiness seeing her. But then, his heart sank.

She was walking hand in hand with a tall, handsome man, heading into the nearby cinema. Arun's breath caught in his throat as he stared, his mind racing. The easy way they walked together, the closeness between them, and the smile on Riya's face... it was too much for him to take in. The sight of her with another man made his chest tighten painfully.

Without thinking, Arun jerked the steering wheel and managed to pull into the cinema's parking lot. His hands were shaking as he parked, his heart pounding in his chest. His thoughts were a blur—*How could this be happening?*—but there was no time to think. He needed answers.

He jumped out of the car, rushing toward the entrance of the theatre. As he reached the door, an officer standing by the entrance stopped him.

"Excuse me, sir. You need a ticket to enter."

Arun's mind was spinning, but he forced himself to stay calm. "Right, sorry," he muttered, quickly buying a ticket. He rushed inside, scanning the hall for any sign of Riya. It didn't take long before he spotted her and the man sitting a few rows ahead, in one of the cozy couple's seats. They were laughing about something, their faces close together, and Arun's stomach churned.

He took a seat nearby, his entire body tense with anger and hurt. His mind was in turmoil—*Why? Why would she do this?* He had trusted her. She had seemed so understanding, so kind. And now this betrayal felt like a knife in his heart.

Arun watched them for a few minutes, his emotions warring inside him. He tried to reason with himself—*maybe it's just a misunderstanding. Maybe it's a friend.* But deep down, he knew what he was seeing. The way they interacted, the casual intimacy between them, was undeniable. Riya wasn't just with any friend—she was with someone else.

His mind flashed back to his father's teachings—about integrity, honesty, and loyalty. Cheating, in any form, was something he could never tolerate. It went against everything he believed in, everything he had been raised to value. Arun clenched his fists, his knuckles white as he tried to contain the surge of anger rising in him.

He couldn't watch any longer.

Without a word, he stood up and walked out of the theatre, his heart pounding in his chest. The cool evening air hit him as he stepped outside, but it did little to soothe the storm brewing inside him. He got into his car, hands gripping the steering wheel tightly, his jaw clenched in frustration.

He couldn't go back to the station just yet—his mind was too distracted. He needed to clear his head, to process what had just happened. He drove aimlessly for a while, thoughts racing.

How could she do this? The question kept repeating in his mind. Arun had never been the type to rush into anything, especially not relationships. He had trusted Riya, believed that she was different. And now, in the span of a few minutes, everything he thought he knew had come crashing down.

Finally, he made his way to the station, parking his car and sitting in silence for a few moments. His heart still ached, but now, beneath the hurt, there was anger. Not just at Riya, but at himself—for being so blind, for letting himself be vulnerable.

As he walked into the station, his colleagues greeted him, but he barely noticed. His mind was elsewhere, consumed by thoughts of Riya and the betrayal he had witnessed. He knew he couldn't let this consume him—he had work to do, responsibilities to uphold. But how could he move forward with this weight pressing down on him?

That night, after a long day at work, Arun found himself sitting in his room, staring at his phone. His mind drifted to Neha, his sister. She always had a way of seeing things from a different perspective, of offering advice when he needed it most.

He dialed her number.

"Hey, Neha," he said when she picked up. His voice sounded heavier than usual, and Neha picked up on it immediately.

"Arun? What's wrong?" she asked, her tone concerned.

Arun hesitated, unsure of where to begin. "I... I saw Riya today."

"Oh? That's great! Did you finally get some time to meet her?" Neha asked, her voice bright.

"No," Arun replied, his tone darkening. "She was with someone else."

There was a pause on the other end. "What do you mean?" Neha asked cautiously.

"I saw her with another guy," Arun explained, his voice tight with emotion. "They were holding hands, laughing together, like... like they were a couple."

Neha sighed. "Arun, maybe it's not what you think. You know how busy you've been with work. It's possible she's just hanging out with a friend."

Arun shook his head, even though Neha couldn't see him. "It didn't look like that, Neha. I've never seen her like that with me."

There was a brief silence before Neha spoke again, her voice softer now. "Look, I know this hurts. But before you jump to conclusions, maybe you should talk to her. Find out what's really going on. Don't assume the worst just yet."

Arun rubbed his forehead, feeling the weight of Neha's words. "Maybe. But it's hard to shake off what I saw. I don't think I can look at her the same way."

Neha sighed on the other end. "I get it, Arun. But you've always been someone who values honesty. So be honest with her. Ask her directly, and see what she has to say."

Arun nodded, knowing that Neha was right. But the hurt, the anger—it wasn't something that would go away easily.

"Thanks, Neha," he said softly. "I'll think about it."

"Take care, Arun. And remember, I'm always here if you need to talk," Neha replied warmly.

As he hung up the phone, Arun sat in the darkness of his room, the memory of Riya and the other man still fresh in his mind. He knew he needed to confront her, to find out the truth. But right now, all he felt was the sharp sting of betrayal.

And that was something he wasn't sure he could ever forgive.

Chapter 7: The Weight of Pride

Arun's pride was a fortress, tall and impenetrable. Even though Neha's words lingered in his mind—telling him to confront Riya, to ask her for the truth—he couldn't bring himself to dial her number. Every time he picked up the phone, his hand hovered over her name, but the bitterness that had lodged itself in his chest refused to let him go any further. He couldn't shake the image of her with the other man. It was like a thorn stuck deep in his heart.

How could she? He kept asking himself. The anger simmered within him, not as explosive as before, but now settled into a quiet, smoldering resentment. Cheating was unforgivable in his eyes, and no explanation would ever change that. Arun was a man of principles, much like his father. He had been raised to value loyalty, and now, he felt like he had been played for a fool.

Days passed, and with each one, the distance between him and Riya grew wider. He started thinking back to their last few conversations. It was subtle, but in hindsight, it was clear to him that something had shifted. When he had ended their calls abruptly due to work, Riya hadn't protested like she used to. She hadn't asked for more time or tried to prolong the conversation. At the time, he had appreciated her understanding, thinking she was mature enough to realize how important his career was to him.

But now, as he replayed those moments in his mind, it seemed less like understanding and more like indifference.

Maybe she had already moved on, he thought bitterly. *Maybe that's why she didn't seem to care.*

He convinced himself that ignoring her was the best course of action. If she could be with someone else so easily, then why should he bother? The hurt was still raw, but his pride shielded him from feeling it too deeply. Arun decided he wouldn't chase her. If Riya didn't care enough to explain herself or even reach out to him after their silence stretched on, then why should he make the effort?

Weeks passed, and to his surprise, she never called. The void left by her absence became more noticeable, but still, his pride wouldn't let him relent. Instead, Arun threw himself into his work, determined to bury his emotions under the weight of his responsibilities. He had always been ambitious, but now that ambition took on a new urgency. His mind was consumed by thoughts of his career and his vision of rising to a higher rank in a short period of time.

At the police station, Arun's performance became exemplary. He took on more cases, volunteered for extra shifts, and earned the admiration of his superiors. His focus was sharp, his resolve unshakable. The ache in his chest from Riya's betrayal was still there, but it was dulled by the satisfaction of his growing accomplishments.

His father, proud of his son's dedication, often praised him during their evening conversations.

"You're doing well, Arun," his father would say, leaning back in his chair after dinner. "I always knew you had the potential to be great. Keep at it, and soon enough, you'll be wearing those stars on your shoulder."

Arun would nod, his jaw set with determination. "That's the plan, Dad."

His father's approval fueled him further. Arun's world had shrunk to the size of his career, and in some ways, it was a relief. The constant bustle of work, the camaraderie with his colleagues, and the sense of purpose kept him too busy to dwell on Riya—or at least that's what he told himself.

But in the quiet moments, when he was alone in his room at night, the memories crept back in. He thought about the late-night calls that had stretched into the early hours, the easy laughter they had shared, and the way Riya's voice had once been a source of comfort. Now, all of that felt like a distant dream, tainted by betrayal.

Despite everything, Arun couldn't completely push her out of his mind. He didn't understand why she had acted the way she did. He could have asked her for answers, but his pride stopped him. He didn't want to show how much she had hurt him, didn't want her to see his pain or weakness. So, he kept a wall between them, refusing to let her know just how much he still cared.

As more time passed, Riya became a ghost in his life. There were no calls, no messages, and no attempts at reconciliation from her side. And that, more than anything, stung. Arun had expected something—an apology, an explanation, maybe even a fight—but instead, there was only silence.

This silence, though, was a double-edged sword. It allowed him to focus entirely on his ambitions, but it also left him wondering. *Had she ever really cared at all?*

Arun's father continued to express his pride in him, and his colleagues admired his work ethic. On the surface, everything seemed to be falling into place. But deep down, Arun knew that something important was missing. He had always envisioned a future where his career and his personal life could coexist, where he could find success and still have someone by his side. But now, that vision seemed fractured.

One evening, as Arun sat at his desk, reviewing paperwork for a new case, he felt the familiar pang of loneliness that had become all too common. He glanced at his phone, her name still sitting in his contacts. For a brief moment, he considered calling her—just to hear her voice, just to ask why.

But he pushed the thought aside.

No, he told himself firmly. *She doesn't deserve that.*

And so, as the night wore on, Arun buried himself deeper into his work, convinced that the only way to heal was to keep moving forward, no matter how much his heart ached in the quiet moments.

Chapter 8: A Meeting at Parkview

Arun stared at the message on his phone for what felt like an eternity. His mind was racing. It had been months since he last heard from Riya, and after what he had witnessed outside the cinema, he thought he'd never see her again. Yet, here she was, asking to meet.

For a moment, he considered deleting the message, pretending he'd never seen it. *What could she possibly want now?* He thought. But then Neha's voice echoed in his mind, *"Sometimes, people have reasons for what they do, Arun. You should at least hear them out."*

With a deep sigh, he typed a simple reply: "Okay, 11 am."

He quickly dressed in a casual suit, not too formal but appropriate enough for what could be an awkward encounter. His heart wasn't racing like it used to when he was on his way to meet her. Instead, there was a heaviness in his chest, a dull ache that reminded him of the betrayal he hadn't yet fully processed.

As he drove to Parkview Restaurant, his thoughts were all over the place. *What could she say to make this right? Why now?* He tried to push the questions away, focusing on the road, but they kept coming back.

By the time he reached the restaurant, it was almost 11. Arun parked the car and took a deep breath before walking inside. The place was as he remembered—charming and quaint, with soft music playing in the background. He spotted Riya sitting at a corner table by the window, her eyes scanning the entrance. She looked just as beautiful as she always had, but there was something different about her. Maybe it was the way her shoulders slumped slightly, or the way her eyes lacked their usual sparkle.

He approached the table slowly, every step feeling heavier than the last.

"Hi, Arun," Riya said softly as he reached the table.

"Hi," he replied, his voice neutral. He pulled out the chair and sat down across from her, keeping his gaze steady.

There was an uncomfortable silence between them. The air felt thick with unspoken words, and Arun had no intention of breaking it first. He wasn't here to make this easy for her. If she had something to say, she could say it.

Riya shifted nervously in her seat, her fingers fidgeting with the edge of her napkin. After a long pause, she finally spoke.

"I'm sure you've been wondering about my silence, Arun," she started softly, her voice trembling. "I don't blame you for that. I... I never intended for things to end up this way."

Arun raised an eyebrow, still not saying anything. He wasn't going to make this easier by filling the silence.

Riya looked down at the table for a moment, gathering her thoughts before continuing. "There's something I never told you. When we started seeing each other, I didn't think it would matter because I thought it was over... but it wasn't." She glanced up at him, searching his face for a sign that he understood, but Arun's expression remained unreadable.

She took a deep breath. "There was someone before you. My first love."

Arun's jaw tightened, but he kept quiet.

"He moved abroad for his studies right before we met," Riya continued, her voice trembling slightly. "We had broken up, or at least I thought we had. He said he needed to focus on his future, and I thought that was the end of it. "That's when I met you, and... I truly fell for you, Arun. I wasn't pretending about that."

Arun's chest tightened. He had a feeling he knew where this was going.

"But then," Riya's voice wavered, "he came back."

Arun felt a coldness settle over him. His fingers clenched slightly around the edge of the table, but he still said nothing.

Riya's eyes were glistening now. "When I saw him again, all those old feelings came rushing back. He told me he wanted to marry me and take me with him when he goes back abroad. I was so confused. I didn't know what to do. You were busy with your work, and I didn't want to hurt you, but I couldn't avoid what was happening. I was torn between the two of you."

Arun could feel his pulse quickening, but he remained silent. His pride wouldn't let him speak.

"I know I messed up," Riya said, her voice shaking. "I should have been honest with you from the start, but I was afraid. Afraid of losing you, and of making the wrong decision."

Arun's throat felt tight, but he finally spoke. "So, what now? Are you with him?" His voice was cold, distant.

Riya nodded slowly. "Yes. We're getting married next month. I wanted to tell you in person because... you deserved to hear it from me."

Arun stared at her, his mind spinning. A part of him had already guessed this would be the outcome, but hearing it confirmed was like a punch to the gut. He swallowed hard, trying to keep his emotions in check.

"And you thought telling me would make this better?" he asked, his tone sharp.

Riya winced at his words. "No, I just... I couldn't leave things like they were. I didn't want you to think that it was all a lie. What we had, it was real. I cared about you, Arun. I still do. But... he was my first love. I guess I never really let him go."

Arun leaned back in his chair, his heart heavy with a mix of anger, sadness, and disappointment. "I wish you had told me earlier, Riya," he said quietly. "I could have handled the truth, but not like this."

"I know," she whispered. "I'm so sorry."

The silence between them stretched out once more, but this time it felt final. Arun realized there was nothing left to say. Riya had made her choice, and now he had to live with the consequences.

He stood up slowly, pushing his chair back. "I hope you're happy with him," he said, his voice steady but cold. "Goodbye, Riya."

Riya looked up at him, tears brimming in her eyes. "Goodbye, Arun."

Without another word, Arun turned and walked out of the restaurant. The weight in his chest felt heavier than ever, but he knew this was the end. There was no going back now. He had to let her go, even if it hurt more than he could bear.

Chapter 9: A New Beginning

Arun tried his best to move on from the past, throwing himself into his work at the police station. The busyness of his daily tasks helped keep his mind off the hurt caused by Riya. It was difficult at first, but over time, the sting of betrayal started to fade. His days were full, and the pressures of the job kept him focused on what really mattered—his career.

One afternoon, as he sat at his desk with a cup of tea, his phone rang. The name on the screen caught his attention immediately: Head Office. He quickly straightened up and answered the call.

"Hello, Arun speaking."

"Arun, this is the IGP's office. The Inspector General would like to have a word with you," the voice on the other end said formally.

Arun felt his heart skip a beat. He had heard rumors about upcoming promotions, but he hadn't expected anything so soon. The phone clicked, and the IGP came on the line.

"Arun, how are you doing?" the IGP's deep, authoritative voice came through.

"I'm doing well, sir. Thank you," Arun responded, keeping his tone respectful but casual.

"I've been hearing good things about you, young man. Your work ethic and dedication have been noticed."

Arun smiled, feeling a swell of pride. "Thank you, sir. I just do my best to serve."

"Well, your best is about to be rewarded," the IGP continued. "We've decided to promote you to the rank of Assistant Superintendent of Police. Congratulations, Arun. You've earned it."

Arun felt a rush of excitement, but before he could respond, the IGP added something unexpected.

"And with this promotion comes a transfer. You'll be assigned to the Willow Brook Police Station in the area where you grew up. It's a fairly big station, but we believe you're ready to handle the responsibility."

Arun was caught off guard. The village? His mind raced as memories of his childhood flashed before him. The quiet streets, the familiar faces, the simplicity of life there. It wasn't what he had expected, but it also wasn't something he could refuse.

"I... I'm honored, sir," Arun finally managed to say. "Thank you for the promotion and the trust. It will be difficult to leave home, but I'm ready to serve wherever I'm needed."

"That's the spirit, Arun," the IGP replied, pleased with his response. "We need officers who are committed to their work, no matter the location. I'm sure you'll make a positive impact there."

Arun took a deep breath, knowing that this was a huge step in his career. "I promise to give my best, sir. I'll uphold the standards of the force and do my duty to the fullest."

"I'm sure you will," the IGP said. "You're expected to report in two weeks. Make the necessary arrangements and keep up the good work."

"Thank you, sir," Arun said with gratitude, his voice firm and confident. "I won't let you down."

The call ended, and Arun sat back in his chair, processing the news. He had just been promoted, which was a dream come true, but the idea of leaving his parents and the familiarity of the city gave him a sense of bittersweet emotion. He knew this was an important step, both personally and professionally, but it also meant parting ways with the life he had built here.

He picked up the phone and dialed his father.

"Dad, you won't believe this," Arun said, his voice unable to hide the excitement.

"What is it, son?" his father asked, sounding curious.

"I've been promoted to Assistant Superintendent. But there's more—I'm being transferred to the Willow Brook Police Station, back where we used to live."

There was a pause on the line before his father's proud voice broke through. "That's fantastic news, Arun! I'm so proud of you. You've worked so hard for this."

"I know, but leaving home won't be easy," Arun admitted. "I'll miss you, mom, Neha and the city life."

"You're doing what you're meant to do, son," his father reassured him. "This is your career, and sometimes it means making sacrifices it'll be good for you to go back, and I'm sure your mother will be thrilled."

After a few more words of encouragement, Arun ended the call and immediately dialed Neha. His sister picked up on the second ring.

"What's up, big brother?" she asked playfully.

"You won't believe this—I've been promoted and transferred to the Willow Brook Police Station," Arun announced, his excitement bubbling over.

"No way! That's awesome!" Neha exclaimed. "You're going to be an Assistant Superintendent? Wow, that's a big deal!"

"Yeah, but it also means moving out of the house. I'll be heading back to Willow Brook soon."

Neha paused for a moment, then her voice softened. "I know it's hard to leave home, Arun, but this is a huge opportunity. And it's our birthplace! I'll definitely visit you. Besides, you'll get to relive all those childhood memories."

Arun chuckled, feeling some of his anxiety ease. "You're right. I'm excited, but nervous at the same time."

"Don't worry," Neha said warmly. "You've got this. You're going to do amazing things, and I'll be there cheering you on. Just think of it as a new chapter."

"Thanks, Neha," Arun replied, feeling grateful for her support. "I'll let you know once I'm settled in. Maybe we can have a family reunion there."

Neha laughed. "That sounds perfect! And hey, don't forget to take care of yourself. It's going to be a big change."

"I won't," Arun assured her. "I'm ready for it."

As Arun ended the call, a mix of emotions swirled inside him—excitement for the promotion, nostalgia for his childhood, and anticipation for what lay ahead. The future was uncertain, but Arun knew one thing for sure: he was ready to embrace whatever came his way.

Chapter 10: Preparing for the New ASP

It was an unusually busy morning at the Willow Brook Police Station. The constables were bustling around, polishing furniture, arranging files, and sweeping every corner in preparation for the arrival of the new ASP, Mr. Arun Fernandez. The excitement was palpable, and everyone seemed to be working twice as fast as usual.

"Ah, I've never seen this place so clean in my life!" joked Constable Raman, wiping sweat from his brow as he pushed a mop across the floor.

"Careful, Raman," teased Constable Prakash, who was dusting the bookshelf. "The new ASP might be able to see his reflection in that floor. You don't want to blind him with the shine!"

The room erupted into laughter, lightening the mood despite the work.

"All jokes aside," said Constable Singh, more serious as he adjusted his cap. "I hear he's a sharp guy, a real no-nonsense officer. We'd better make sure everything's perfect. Last thing we need is for him to walk in and trip over a pile of reports."

"I heard he's originally from Willow Brook," piped up one of the younger officers, Constable Mohan, as he straightened up the bulletin board. "I bet he'll be one of those types who cares about the people here. That means he'll care about us too, right?"

OIC (Officer in Charge) Inspector Deshmukh entered the station with a clipboard in hand, surveying the preparations with a watchful eye. He was known for his no-nonsense attitude, but even he couldn't hide a hint of pride at how everyone was pulling together.

"Good work, everyone," Deshmukh said, nodding approvingly. "The ASP will be arriving shortly, and I want everything to go smoothly. He's young but experienced, and I expect you all to make him feel welcome."

Raman, still with his mop, glanced at Prakash and smirked. "Well, maybe if we keep this place spotless, he'll be so impressed he'll let us take an extra tea break."

"Dream on, Raman," Prakash laughed. "You'll be lucky if he doesn't have us working double shifts with that attitude."

As they chatted, Constable Kumar was meticulously arranging some paperwork at the front desk, making sure everything was in order.

"Do you think he'll be strict?" Kumar asked no one in particular.

"Of course, he will," Prakash responded, his tone mock-serious. "That's why we have to make sure everything is perfect. You don't want to be on the wrong side of a new boss, especially when he's got the power to shake things up."

"Stop with the gossiping and focus on your work," Deshmukh said, though there was a faint smile on his lips. "Remember, we represent this station. We'll give him a proper welcome, and show him that this team works like a well-oiled machine."

By the time Arun's jeep arrived at the station, everything was in place. The station looked spotless, the staff were neatly in uniform, and the officers stood in formation, ready to greet him. Arun stepped out of the vehicle, his eyes scanning the familiar village surroundings before landing on the station's entrance.

Deshmukh stepped forward to greet him, his hand outstretched.

"Welcome, sir," Deshmukh said with a respectful nod. "It's an honor to have you as our new ASP. We've been expecting you."

Arun smiled and shook his hand firmly. "Thank you, Inspector Deshmukh. It's good to be back in my hometown. I look forward to working with all of you."

The constables stood at attention as Arun entered the station, trying their best to appear professional, though the tension of first impressions was still thick in the air. Arun took a moment to glance around, nodding approvingly at the tidiness.

"You've done a great job with the station," Arun remarked, his tone friendly but authoritative. "I can see the team here takes pride in their work. I'm sure we'll make a strong team together."

"Absolutely, sir," Deshmukh responded, motioning towards the officers. "Everyone here is dedicated. We work hard, but we also know how to support each other."

Arun chuckled lightly. "That's exactly what I like to hear. Now, let's get to work and make this place even better."

As the officers returned to their duties, Raman whispered to Prakash, "You think he noticed how shiny the floor is?"

Prakash stifled a laugh. "Shut up, Raman. You'll get us both in trouble."

The rest of the day was filled with introductions, Arun getting to know each of the officers personally. Despite the lighthearted moments, there was a sense of respect in the air. The team felt relieved that their new ASP was approachable yet professional, and they couldn't help but feel optimistic about the days ahead.

Arun felt the same. Despite the weight of responsibility on his shoulders, he was excited to be back in his village and ready to make a difference. As he stood in his new office, looking out over the familiar village he once called home, he knew this was just the beginning of something important.

Chapter 11: A Journey Down Memory Lane

After weeks of settling into his new role at the village police station, Arun finally had a day off. It had been years since he last explored the familiar surroundings of his childhood. The idea of revisiting those old places stirred a deep sense of nostalgia. His thoughts kept drifting to Meera, the dear cute little friend who had once been such a big part of his and Neha's lives. He was fairly certain her family had moved away long ago, but something inside him tugged at the idea of going back, just to see the place again. Maybe, in some way, it would still hold traces of her.

Arun dressed casually for the day, choosing comfortable attire that allowed him to blend in as just another villager. As he drove through the streets, he marveled at how much the village had changed. What was once a sleepy, rural area had transformed into a more modernized settlement. Newly built houses lined the freshly tarred roads, and Arun found himself slightly disoriented, searching for familiar landmarks.

His heart sank a little when he reached the spot where his childhood home once stood. In its place was a brand-new structure, gleaming with fresh paint. Time had moved on, and so had his old house. Yet, just next door, Meera's house still stood, though renovated with a fresh coat of paint and an extended porch. The frame of the house was the same, though, and it brought back a flood of memories.

With some hesitation, Arun parked his car and walked up to the familiar garden. The flowers in the yard had changed, but the sense of comfort remained. He tapped gently on the door, unsure of what to expect. The sound of footsteps approaching the door made his heart quicken.

When the door opened, a mature lady stood before him. She looked older, but her face carried the same warmth he remembered. "Aunty Martha, can you recognize me?" Arun asked, smiling gently.

The woman stared at him, her brow furrowing slightly as she scrutinized his face. And then, a wide smile broke across her features, eyes lighting up with realization. "My God, this is Arun, isn't it?"

"Yes, Aunty," Arun replied, stepping forward as she reached out to embrace him. "It's me, all grown up."

"Come in, dear! Come in! It's been years. Look at you!" Aunty Martha pulled him inside, her excitement palpable. "I can't believe you're back."

As they sat down in the cozy living room, filled with the familiar scent of home, they began reminiscing about the old days. The warmth of her voice, the gentle hum of the ceiling fan, everything felt just as it had in his childhood. Arun was flooded with memories, and he found himself at ease, happy to be back in this part of his life.

Just then, the sound of soft footsteps echoed from the hallway. Arun turned, and his breath caught in his throat. A young girl, perhaps no older than eighteen, stepped into the room holding a book. Her flowing hair cascaded gently around her face, catching the sunlight that streamed through the window. Her skin glowed with a natural radiance, and every movement she made exuded a quiet grace. She was captivating, her beauty pure and untouched, with an innocence that made her even more enchanting. She glanced at her mother, then at Arun, her eyes silently questioning. Martha turned to her daughter with a smile. "Do you recognize him? This is Arun, the boy who used to live next door. You've heard me talk about him before."

The girl looked at Arun for a moment, then turned to her mother with a soft smile. "Yes, Mom, I remember you mentioning someone named Arun, but his face isn't very clear in my memory. I'm sorry. Martha smiled warmly and said, "Yes, dear, that's understandable. You were barely four when they left Willow Brook."

Arun was caught off guard, momentarily speechless. He hadn't expected to be so profoundly affected by anyone today, let alone by someone as stunning as this young woman. Her beauty was genuine and natural, exuding a charm that felt refreshingly untouched by the complexities of the modern world. There was an elegance in her simplicity that disarmed him completely. As his heart raced, he steeled himself, reminding himself to stay calm and grounded, as was expected of someone in his esteemed position.

"It's okay," Arun said, managing to smile back at her. "I guess I've changed a lot since then."

The girl gave a soft, shy laugh, her eyes meeting his briefly before glancing away. There was an innocence in her manner that Arun found endearing. She moved with a grace that was mesmerizing, and it was clear she was a person of both beauty and kindness.

"Meera," Martha called to her daughter, "why don't you bring some tea and snacks for our guest?"

"Of course, Mom," Meera replied, slipping out of the room as gracefully as she had entered.

Arun watched her leave, his thoughts momentarily scattered. He hadn't expected this visit to stir up such feelings. What was meant to be a simple trip down memory lane had turned into something more—something unexpected.

"You're lucky, Arun," Martha said, bringing his attention back to the conversation. "Not many people get to come back to their childhood home. So much has changed, but I'm glad you're here. And it seems like you've done well for yourself."

"Yes, Aunty," Arun replied, trying to regain his composure. "Life has been busy, but I've been fortunate."

Arun inquired, "Is Uncle George here? I was hoping to speak with him."

Martha responded, "He's gone to town for the day. He'll be back a little later."

Martha smiled warmly. "Well, it's good to see you back, Arun. And Meera—she's our pride and joy. She's studying literature, you know. Quite the reader, just like you were."

Arun nodded, though his mind kept drifting back to Meera's captivating presence. This visit had brought him more than just a trip down memory lane. It had given him something he hadn't expected—a connection to his past, and perhaps, the spark of something new.

When Meera returned with a tray of tea and snacks, she smiled shyly at Arun as she carefully set it down before taking a seat across from him. As they sat together, sipping tea and enjoying the snacks, Arun found himself stealing glances at her. She radiated a timeless beauty, her gentle demeanor and authentic charm captivating him..

As the conversation continued, Arun found himself caught between the memories of his childhood and the new, stirring emotions he hadn't anticipated. His heart, once hardened by past disappointments, felt something unfamiliar again—a quiet hope.

Chapter 12: Unspoken Emotions

Meera couldn't shake the feeling that had settled in her heart ever since Arun left that afternoon. Her usually peaceful thoughts were now in turmoil. The way he had smiled at her, how his eyes lingered, left an impression that was far deeper than any fleeting crush she had ever experienced. The boys in her college, her classmates, and even those who tried to catch her attention felt insignificant compared to Arun's commanding presence. Despite their age difference, it was his maturity and quiet dignity that stirred emotions within her that she couldn't quite explain. Age was just a number; the connection she felt with him was undeniable and profound.

After helping her mother clean up the dishes, Meera casually asked, "Mom, how old was Arun when they left the village?"

Her mother paused, wiping her hands on a dish towel, and looked at her daughter with a curious smile. "Well, sweetie, he was about 14, and you were only 4. It's hard to believe you'd remember anything from that time."

"I don't really recall much," Meera admitted, her voice trailing off as she gazed out the window. "It just feels... strange, you know? Hearing so much about him and now seeing him again after all these years."

Martha chuckled softly, a twinkle in her eye as she noticed the thoughtful look on her daughter's face. "He has certainly grown into a fine man. But don't get too carried away with old memories, darling. Life is always moving forward."

Later, when George returned home, Martha excitedly filled him in on Arun's visit. "Can you believe it? The new ASP, Arun, is none other than the boy who grew up next door!"

Her father's eyebrows shot up in surprise. "Arun? Little Arun? He's the ASP now?" He shook his head in amazement. "Time flies, doesn't it? Seems like just yesterday the kids were running around in this yard."

But Meera wasn't paying attention. Her thoughts drifted away, consumed by the image of Arun seated in their living room, engaged in conversation with her mother. That night, as she lay in bed staring at the ceiling, sleep eluded her. Her heart raced as she replayed the moments of the afternoon in her mind. Arun's steady gaze, the way he spoke with calm authority, and the subtle smile that danced at the corners of his lips—it all captivated her. The admiration she felt for him was unlike the innocent attention she received from boys her own age; it was something deeper, something intense.

Meanwhile, in Arun's quarters...

As soon as Arun reached his quarters, he immediately pulled out his phone and dialed Neha. His mind was full of thoughts of Meera, and he needed to talk to someone about it.

"Hello, Arun!" Neha answered cheerfully. "How's the village treating you?"

"Neha, you won't believe who I met today," Arun started, his voice still carrying the excitement from his visit.

"Who? Did you run into one of your old school friends?" Neha asked, intrigued.

"No, no... It's something much more interesting," Arun replied, his tone teasing.

"Come on, stop building suspense!" Neha laughed. "Who is it?"

"Meera," Arun murmured, letting the name linger on his lips as if he were tasting something sweet. "Do you remember the little girl who lived next door when we were kids? I stopped by to see Aunty Martha today, and you'll never guess what I found. She's all grown up now, and Neha—oh, you won't believe it—she's absolutely stunning."

There was a moment of silence before Neha spoke up, her voice laced with curiosity. "Stunning, you say? Sounds like there's a little more than just admiration behind those words!"

Arun chuckled, feeling slightly self-conscious. "It's not just that, Neha. She's graceful, calm... there's something about her, something pure. I couldn't stop staring at her."

Neha laughed softly. "Arun, I've never heard you talk about a girl like this before. So, what's the plan? Are you planning to see her again?"

"I'm not sure," Arun replied. "I didn't make any promises. But, Neha, Aunty Martha suggested I bring you along for lunch next weekend. What do you say? You can meet her, and then you can tell me what you think."

"Ahh, so you want me to be the judge of this girl, huh?" Neha teased. "You know I'd love to come, Arun. I'll be there for sure."

"Good," Arun said, relieved. "It's settled then. Next weekend, we'll go to lunch, and maybe—just maybe—you can help me figure out what's going on in my head."

Neha's laughter rang through the phone. "Oh, Arun. Always overthinking. But I'll be there, don't worry. And for what it's worth, it sounds like this girl has already gotten under your skin."

Arun leaned back in his chair, his mind drifting back to Meera's shy smile and the way her eyes had sparkled when she looked at him. "Maybe she has, Neha. Maybe she has."

As he ended the call, Arun couldn't help but smile to himself. For the first time in a long while, something other than his career was occupying his mind. He didn't know what the future held, but one thing was certain—Meera had awakened something inside him that he couldn't ignore.

In her room, Meera lay wide awake, staring up at the ceiling, the soft glow of moonlight filtering through the curtains. A whirlwind of emotions swirled inside her, feelings that were both new and overwhelming. Arun had transformed from a childhood memory into a tangible presence in her life once more. The mere thought of him sent delightful shivers through her, leaving her heart fluttering in a way that made sleep impossible. She found herself lost in daydreams, replaying their encounter, each moment more vivid than the last, as the night stretched on.

Chapter 13: Anticipated Gathering

Meera was in the kitchen, carefully rolling out the dough for the fish pie, when she heard her mother call out.

"Meera, my angel!" Martha's voice carried through the house, warm and soothing.

"Yes, Mom?" Meera responded, wiping her hands on her apron as she stepped into the living room.

"I casually told Arun to bring Neha for lunch today," Martha said, watching her daughter's reaction closely. "They might drop in anytime. I sent your father to get some provisions so we can prepare a good meal for them. And I thought... maybe you could make that fish pie? Arun used to love it when he was a boy."

Meera's heart leapt in her chest. "Arun and Neha are coming? For lunch? Today?" she stammered, trying to contain her excitement.

"Yes, dear," Martha smiled knowingly. "And I think it's the perfect opportunity for you to show off your cooking skills."

Meera's face flushed with both excitement and nervousness. "I'll get right to it, Mom! And I'll make sure the house is spotless too."

As Meera returned to the kitchen, her mind raced with thoughts of Arun. Ever since he had visited, she hadn't been able to stop thinking about him. Now, the prospect of seeing him again—so soon—filled her with a sense of anticipation. She imagined him sitting at the table, smiling at her with that same gentle gaze, and it made her heart flutter.

Meanwhile, Martha stood at the window, gazing out thoughtfully. What a nice man Arun has become, she mused. But is my poor angel lucky enough to win his heart? She remembered the way Arun had paid extra attention to Meera the other day, and she couldn't help but wonder if there was something more there. If only... if only it could be that simple. But she also knew how high-minded Arun's father was. Would he approve of a match between them?

Martha sighed, shaking her head at her own thoughts. How foolish of me to think like this after just a couple of hours of meeting. She forced herself to concentrate on her chores, but the thought lingered in the back of her mind.

At Arun's Quarters – Later That Morning

A car pulled into the yard, and Arun, who was sipping his morning coffee, looked up to see Neha stepping out, her arms full of gift parcels. She waved at him excitedly.

"Neha, what's all this?" Arun asked, surprised as he walked over to help her with the packages.

"You silly chap!" Neha teased, laughing as she handed him a box. "Don't you know the customs? You can't show up to lunch empty-handed, especially when you're invited to someone's home. We need to bring gifts and sweets—it's a sign of respect!"

Arun chuckled, shaking his head. "I never thought of that. I guess I'm not very good at these social graces."

"That's why you have me!" Neha winked, nudging him playfully. "I knew you'd forget, so I came prepared."

Arun gave her a warm smile. "I have to admit, you always think ahead. I'd be lost without you."

Neha laughed, placing the last of the boxes in his arms. "Well, that's what sisters are for. Now let's hurry, we don't want to be late."

As they got into the car, Neha couldn't resist teasing him a little more. "So... Meera, huh?" she said with a mischievous grin.

Arun shifted in his seat, trying to act casual. "What about her?"

"Come on, you know what I mean," Neha said, her eyes sparkling with amusement. "You've been talking about her non-stop since your last visit. I can tell you're smitten."

Arun cleared his throat, feeling a bit embarrassed. "I just think she's... different. She's not like the other girls I've met."

"Oh, I see," Neha teased, pretending to be deep in thought. "Not like the others, huh? Is it her beauty, her charm, or something else?"

"It's everything," Arun admitted, a small smile playing on his lips. "There's something pure about her. She's unspoiled by the world, you know? It's refreshing."

Neha raised an eyebrow, genuinely curious. "Well, I'll see for myself soon enough. But Arun, just remember—don't rush into anything. You've barely reconnected with her. Take your time."

"I know," Arun nodded. "But there's something there, Neha. I can feel it."

Neha smiled warmly at her brother. "If anyone deserves happiness, it's you, Arun. Just promise me you'll be careful."

"I promise," he said sincerely. "Now, let's go and make a good impression."

Chapter 14: The First Meeting

Meera was finishing up the last of the household chores when she decided it was time to take a break. Her excitement about the lunch visit from Arun and Neha had been building up since morning, and she knew she wanted to look her best. She headed to the bathroom, feeling the need to relax and gather her thoughts.

As the cool water from the shower cascaded over her, Meera closed her eyes and let herself drift into a daydream. Thoughts of Arun swirled in her mind—the way he had looked at her the other day, the warmth in his eyes, his kind smile. She couldn't help but wonder if he had thought about her as much as she had thought about him.

Once she stepped out of the shower, she felt refreshed, her skin glowing from the warmth of the bath. She picked out her favorite magenta dress, the one her friends had always complimented, saying it enhanced her radiant beauty. As she slipped it on, she caught a glimpse of herself in the mirror. The dress hugged her figure perfectly, and she smiled, feeling confident. She sprayed a light mist of her favorite mild perfume, one that lingered gently in the air, and gave herself a final approving nod.

Just as she was adjusting her hair, she heard the doorbell ring. Her heart skipped a beat. *They're here.*

She rushed out of her room, feeling a wave of excitement as she headed towards the door. Before she could reach it, her father, Mr. George, got there first. He opened the door with a broad smile, and seeing Arun and Neha standing there with gifts in their hands, he welcomed them warmly.

"Arun, my boy!" Mr. George greeted him with a hearty handshake and pulled him into a warm hug. "It's so good to see you after all these years."

"Thank you, Uncle," Arun smiled, returning the hug. "It's great to be back."

"And this must be Neha," Mr. George added, turning to her. "Welcome, my dear."

"Thank you, Uncle," Neha smiled brightly as Mr. George hugged her too.

As they entered the house, Meera emerged from the hallway, her heart racing. Arun's eyes immediately found hers, and for a moment, it was as if everything else faded away. Meera's radiant appearance in the magenta dress made Arun pause, his breath catching slightly. He couldn't help but admire her beauty, the way the dress seemed to glow against her skin, how effortlessly graceful she looked.

"Hello, Meera," Arun said, his voice softer than usual, his eyes locked on hers.

Hi, Arun," Meera said shyly, a blush creeping onto her cheeks. "It's so nice to see you again."

Neha, noticing the sweet interaction, hugged Meera tightly. "You know, Meera, when we were kids, Arun and I used to argue over who could carry you on our backs," she said with a playful grin.

Arun chuckled, leaning against the doorframe. "It's probably for the best! We were both pretty competitive about it."

Neha rolled her eyes, still smiling. "Only because I let you win! But you know I was the strongest!"

Meera smiled widely, her eyes sparkling with delight. "I'm sorry, but I just can't recollect those interesting incidents." She leaned in closer, clearly intrigued. "But it's so much fun to hear about them!"

"Come, come, make yourselves at home," Mr. George said, ushering them into the living room. "Martha has been preparing a feast for you both."

As they settled down, Neha glanced at Arun with a mischievous smile. On their way to Meera's house, they had discussed an idea, and she decided it was the perfect moment to bring it up.

"Uncle, Aunty," Neha began, addressing Mr. and Mrs. George with a warm smile, "we were thinking, how about you and Meera join us next weekend? We could show you around the city—do some shopping, have a nice meal at a restaurant. It would be lovely."

"Oh, that sounds wonderful," Martha said, her eyes lighting up. What do you think, George?"

Mr. George nodded enthusiastically. "It's a great idea! We could use a little getaway."

Arun smiled, but before he could say more, he added, "I'd love to join you, but I've got some work to wrap up on Saturday. I might only be free on Sunday."

Neha, ever the go-getter, chimed in with unwavering confidence. "No worries, Arun! I've got everything covered. I'll handle their transport and ensure they're settled in nicely until you can join us."

Arun chuckled, a hint of admiration in his voice. "I should have guessed you'd already have a plan."

With a playful grin, Neha replied, "You know me—I'm always one step ahead!"

Meera, who had been quietly listening, felt her heart flutter at the thought of spending more time with Arun, even if it was just a casual family outing. She couldn't help but wonder if this was the beginning of something deeper, something she had secretly longed for ever since Arun had returned to her life.

Martha, sensing the growing connection between Arun and Meera, was pleased but cautious. She knew how fragile young hearts could be, and though she saw potential in their budding relationship, she wanted to tread carefully. Still, the idea of Arun becoming part of their family was a comforting thought.

As the afternoon continued, the conversation flowed easily between the families. Arun and Mr. George reminisced about old times, while Neha and Meera chatted about their favorite books and hobbies.

The dining table was modest yet inviting, adorned with a simple checkered tablecloth that brought a touch of homey charm to the gathering. A steaming fish pie sat at the center, its golden crust perfectly baked, surrounded by bowls of fresh garden salad and a basket of homemade bread. The rich aroma wafting through the room reminded everyone of cherished family meals shared in the past.

As they gathered around the table, Arun glanced at the fish pie, a nostalgic smile spreading across his face. "Meera, I can't believe you made this! It smells just like the one your mom used to make when we were kids. It was always my favorite."

Meera beamed at the compliment, her cheeks flushing with warmth. "I'm really glad you remember it! Mom taught me how to make it just like she did."

Martha, serving generous portions to everyone, chimed in with a chuckle. "Arun would always beg for seconds! I think we had to keep an eye on him to make sure he didn't eat all the leftovers before the day was over."

Arun laughed, nodding in agreement. "I couldn't help it! Your cooking was legendary, Aunty Martha.

Neha leaned over to Meera, a playful smile dancing on her lips. "You've really brought back some fond memories, Meera. This fish pie is incredible! It's hard to believe you've turned into such a fantastic cook."

"I just followed Mom's recipe!" Meera replied, her voice brimming with pride. "But I'm happy it reminds you of those times. We had so much fun back then."

"Those were the days," Arun said wistfully, his eyes glinting with nostalgia. "It's nice to reconnect over something so simple yet special."

As they all took their first bites, the table fell into a comfortable silence, broken only by the sounds of enjoyment. The rich flavors of the fish pie filled their mouths, and smiles broke out around the table as they savored the meal.

Arun looked at Meera and said softly, "You really have a gift. This brings back so many good memories."

"Thank you! That means a lot coming from you," Meera replied, her heart swelling with happiness.

As the lunch continued, stories flowed easily, creating a warm atmosphere filled with laughter and shared memories, making the simple meal feel like a feast of connection.

As the evening wore on, and the sun began to set, Arun and Neha said their goodbyes, promising to see them next weekend for their city trip.

"Thank you for having us," Neha said warmly as she hugged Aunty Martha. "We're looking forward to next weekend."

Martha smiled, hugging her back. "So are we, my dear. We'll see you then."

As Arun turned to Meera one last time, their eyes met, and for a moment, it felt as though the world had slowed down. "I'll see you next weekend," he said softly.

"I'll be waiting," Meera replied, her voice barely above a whisper, but filled with meaning.

As Arun and Neha drove away, the air in the house felt lighter, charged with the promise of something new and exciting. Meera watched them leave, her heart full of anticipation for what the future might hold.

Chapter 15: A Sister's Promise

Neha was the kind of sister Arun could always count on, especially when it came to handling delicate matters. After their day at Meera's house, she had sensed what was going on in her brother's heart. Later that night, as they sat in their living room, Arun finally spoke up.

"Neha, I need to thank you," Arun said, his voice full of gratitude. "I don't know what I'd do without you. You're always so organized, so on top of things."

Neha smiled, tilting her head. "Oh, come on. You know I'm just doing what I can. It's obvious you've got a lot going on, with work and... Other things."

Arun chuckled. "You mean Meera?"

"Exactly." Neha's eyes twinkled as she said it. "Look, I can see how much she means to you. And after that lunch, it's pretty clear she's got some feelings for you, too. Don't worry about the logistics of it. I've got your back."

"Logistics?" Arun shook his head, laughing softly. "You talk like this is a military operation."

Neha shrugged. "It kind of is, isn't it? But really, I'll make sure everything goes smoothly. After our city trip next weekend, I'll talk to mom and dad about Meera."

Arun's face softened. "You would do that for me?"

"Of course, you're my brother," Neha replied. "And I want to see you happy. You've always been the one with a tough job, putting others before yourself. Now it's time to focus on what makes you happy."

Arun reached over and squeezed her hand. "I don't know how I got so lucky with you as my sister."

Neha laughed, brushing off the sentimentality with a playful swat at his arm. "Oh, don't get all emotional on me now. Just do your part and let me handle the rest."

Though Arun was skilled in his work as a police officer, he often felt out of his depth when it came to personal matters. Neha had always been the planner in the family, with a natural ability to organize, foresee potential problems, and smooth things over before they escalated. It was something Arun had admired in her for as long as he could remember.

"Maybe you got that from both Mom and Dad," Arun mused aloud. "That sense of organization, being methodical... I've always been more of the 'jump into action' type."

Neha smirked. "Exactly. That's why you need me."

The following week unfolded just as planned. While Arun was busy with work, Neha stepped in effortlessly, arranging for Meera and her parents to travel to the city and meet their family. Everything went smoothly, and nothing interfered with Arun's schedule.

As they all gathered in Neha's parents' cozy living room, the atmosphere was warm and welcoming. Meera's parents and Neha's were deep in conversation, chatting easily about village life, the upcoming harvest, and old neighbors who had recently moved away. Laughter occasionally bubbled up from their corner as they reminisced, lost in their own memories.

Meanwhile, Neha leaned in closer to Meera, a playful glint in her eye. "You wouldn't believe what Arun and I used to get up to as kids," she whispered, clearly about to share something mischievous.

"You know, Meera," she began, her voice low, "there was this one time when Arun and I thought we could fix the garden swing in our backyard?"

"We must've been around 10 and 12, maybe a bit older, and Arun was determined to play the 'handyman.' He grabbed this big toolbox, even though we didn't have a clue how to use most of the tools inside."

Meera's eyes sparkled with amusement as she listened, already knowing where this story was headed. "Oh no, what happened?"

Neha chuckled. "So, Arun was insisting that he knew what he was doing. He kept saying, 'Neha, just hold the swing steady while I fix this bolt.' But of course, the minute he started tightening things, the whole swing collapsed. We both fell flat on the ground, and the swing frame came crashing down right on top of us!"

Meera couldn't help but laugh, imagining the scene. "Did you both get hurt?"

"No, luckily not," Neha grinned, "but our pride sure did! Arun was so embarrassed that he refused to admit it was his fault. He kept blaming me for 'distracting' him, even though he was the one giving all the orders. I teased him about it for weeks. And of course, our mom was furious that we'd ruined her favorite swing."

Meera giggled, her cheeks slightly flushed from laughing so much. "It sounds like you and Arun were quite the troublemakers."

Neha nodded with a wink. "Oh, we were. And the best part? Arun was always trying to act like he was in charge, but things always seemed to go wrong when he did."

Meera smiled, feeling a sense of warmth from the stories. Though she couldn't remember much of Arun and Neha from when she was little, hearing about their playful sibling rivalry made her feel even more connected to them.

"You wouldn't believe it, but he was always so competitive with me," Neha added with a laugh. "Everything was a challenge—who could climb the highest tree, who could run the fastest. And of course, he never let me win without a fight."

Meera's laughter bubbled up again, and she shook her head. "It's fun hearing all of this, even if I don't remember any of it. You two must've been so entertaining to watch!"

Neha leaned back, grinning. "Oh, we definitely kept our parents on their toes."

As the evening wore on, Neha's stories kept Meera laughing and feeling more and more at ease. The warmth of the conversation and the shared moments made Meera feel a deep connection with Arun's family, as if she were already part of them.

Finally, as the night drew to a close and Meera was helping clear away the dishes, Neha approached her with a more serious tone. She glanced around to make sure they had a moment alone before she spoke.

"So, Meera," Neha began softly, "I've noticed the way you and Arun look at each other."

Meera froze for a moment, her heart pounding. She wasn't sure how to respond, but Neha's gentle smile put her at ease.

"It's okay," Neha reassured her. "I just wanted to know... what do you think about Arun?"

Meera hesitated, unsure if she should reveal her true feelings. But there was something about Neha's kindness and openness that made her feel safe to share.

"I don't know," Meera finally said, her voice barely above a whisper. "I've been thinking about him a lot since we met again. He's... different from anyone I've known. I don't really know how to explain it."

Neha smiled knowingly. "You don't have to. I can see it. And for what it's worth, I think he feels the same way about you."

Meera's heart fluttered at the thought. "Do you really think so?"

"I do," Neha said confidently. "And if you ever need to talk about it, I'm here. Just know that whatever happens, you're already important to him."

Meera blushed, feeling a wave of emotions she hadn't expected. She had always admired Arun from afar, but hearing Neha's words made everything feel more real, more possible.

As they finished tidying up, Meera couldn't help but smile to herself. The idea of Arun returning her feelings was both thrilling and terrifying. But with Neha's support, she felt more confident than ever that something beautiful could come from it.

Later that night, as Neha lay in bed, she couldn't help but smile at the day's events. She had always known her brother to be a good man, but seeing him with Meera, she realized just how much love and care he was capable of. It was time for Arun to be happy, and if Meera was the one to make that happen, then Neha would do everything in her power to support them.

And with that thought, Neha drifted off to sleep, excited for the future that was slowly but surely unfolding.

Chapter 16: A Promise in the Air

Arun woke up to the sound of his phone buzzing on the bedside table. It was Neha. Groggily, he answered the call, still settling back against his pillow.

"Your judgment was correct!" Neha's voice chimed through the line.

Arun blinked, rubbing his eyes. "What judgment are you talking about?" he asked, still half-asleep.

"Meera. She's unspoiled, genuine," Neha replied. "You were her first love, apparently."

Arun's expression shifted, his interest piqued. "Is that so?" He leaned back, a subtle, satisfied smile spreading across his face.

"Yes! You've got nothing to worry about. She's completely smitten," Neha teased.

Arun's smile grew, a sense of relief settling over him. "That's good to hear."

"By the way," Neha interrupted, "what time are you leaving? We're waiting for you."

"Give me an hour, and I'll be on my way."

"Alright, lazy chap, don't keep us waiting too long. See you soon." And with that, the call ended.

At Neha's house, the morning air was filled with anticipation. Meera, though outwardly calm, was brimming with impatience. She wanted to ask Neha if Arun would arrive by noon or later, but her shyness kept her silent. Her heart raced at the thought of seeing him again.

As if reading her mind, Neha came to the breakfast table, grinning. "That lazy chap has just woken up. He'll be here in about an hour," she said, settling into her chair. "We should have lunch here and then go out for dinner with him."

Meera's heart skipped a beat at the thought of spending the entire afternoon and evening with Arun. She smiled softly to herself, feeling a sense of relief.

On his way, following Neha's suggestion, Arun stopped by a store and picked up an expensive perfume and a box of chocolates. He was eager to give these gifts to Meera, knowing he wouldn't have a chance tomorrow since Arun had to report back to the police station early the next morning, but he also needed to drop Meera and her family at their home in Willow Brook. Now, all he had to do was find the perfect moment to give them to her before the day ended. When Arun finally arrived at the house, he noticed the women were busy in the kitchen, preparing lunch, while Meera's father and Neha's father were deep in conversation, discussing the latest political issues. Arun greeted the men briefly before heading into the kitchen, where he saw Meera chopping vegetables, laughing at something Neha had said.

When Meera noticed him, her face lit up, her eyes shining with happiness. The air between them felt charged, though they hadn't said a word yet.

"Hey, Arun!" Neha said, smirking. "You look too formal for someone who just woke up!"

Arun grinned. "Had to freshen up for this feast you're preparing." His gaze shifted to Meera, who looked down shyly, a faint blush spreading across her cheeks.

After a quick wash and a change into a light suit, Arun rejoined the group. Some of the family had gathered to play a casual game of carom, while Meera sat in a corner, absorbed in a book. Arun glanced around and thought this might be the perfect time to talk to her privately.

With a deliberate loudness in his voice, he called across the room, "You seem to be a bit of a bookworm, Meera. Come on, I'll show you my library upstairs. You can pick out some good books."

Meera looked up from her book, slightly flustered but intrigued. She hesitated for a moment, then nodded. "Okay, I'd love that."

As they walked upstairs, Arun couldn't help but notice how radiant Meera looked in her pink dress. The color made her glow, and the soft scent of her perfume filled the air around them.

Once in the library, Arun casually led her around the room, pointing out a few of his favorite books. "I've always been fascinated by history and politics," he said, pulling out a worn hardcover. "What about you? Do you think you could ever enjoy city life?"

Meera, still shy, smiled. "The city seems exciting, but I think I'm more attached to the peace of village life. There's something calming about it. But I wouldn't mind exploring the city more, especially with someone who knows it well."

Arun smiled, feeling more at ease. "Well, the city has its charms. I think you'd grow to love it." He paused, looking deeply into her eyes. Slowly, he reached into his pocket and pulled out the perfume and chocolate, holding them out to her.

Meera blinked in surprise. "What's this?" she asked, her eyes wide.

Arun's voice took on a calm, steady tone, reflecting the weight of his words and the responsibility he carried in his life. "Meera," he began, his gaze sincere, "there's something I've wanted to express for a while now. From the first moment I saw you again, something shifted in me. I didn't fully understand it then, but I realize now—it was more than just a passing feeling. I've come to care for you deeply, not just as a memory from the past, but as someone I want to stand by, protect, and cherish. My feelings for you are genuine, and I would be honored to share my life with you, if you feel the same."

Meera stood there, speechless for a moment. She clutched the gifts in her hands, her heart pounding. Her gaze met Arun's, and in that instant, all the feelings she'd been holding back came rushing to the surface.

"I... I don't know what to say," Meera whispered, her voice trembling. "But... Arun, I've felt the same way since the day I saw you. My heart knew, even before my mind could catch up. I love you. I've never felt this way before, and I know you're the one."

There was a long, quiet moment as the two stood facing each other, the weight of their words settling between them. Arun gently cupped her face and kissed her forehead, a tender, reassuring gesture. "I promise," he said softly, "I'll keep you safe, and I'll love you until my last breath. Believe me."

Meera's heart swelled, her emotions too overwhelming to put into words. She simply nodded, her eyes filled with unshed tears of happiness. Arun took her hand in his, and together, they stood there in the quiet, knowing that this was the beginning of something beautiful, something real.

They lingered in that moment, a promise shared silently between them, as the warmth of their newfound love wrapped around them like a soft, comforting blanket.

Chapter 17: A Day to Remember

After a fun-filled day of shopping, laughter, and a delicious dinner with Meera's family and Neha, they finally made it back home—well past midnight. The day had been an adventure, overflowing with joy and lighthearted moments. They strolled through the bustling malls, where Neha couldn't resist teasing Arun for his questionable fashion choices. "Arun, really? How do you manage to look this good without knowing anything about style?" she joked, earning a playful eye roll from him.

Meera's parents, on the other hand, were wide-eyed, amazed by the bright city stores and modern designs they'd never seen before. Arun had everyone in stitches when Meera stood frozen in front of two almost identical scarves, unable to pick. "Come on, Meera!" Arun laughed, "You're really going to debate over two scarves that look the same?"

Meera pouted playfully, making everyone burst out laughing. The day had been one to remember, full of warmth and good-natured fun.

At the restaurant, the mood remained light and cheerful. They enjoyed a delicious meal, with Meera shyly complimenting Arun on his food choices. Neha, being her usual witty self, cracked jokes about Arun's quiet nature, even as he rolled his eyes playfully. Meera's father joined in with funny stories from his own youth, causing bursts of laughter around the table. At one point, the waiter had mistakenly brought out the wrong dish, and the confusion that followed turned into a funny incident, with everyone in stitches by the end of it.

When they returned home, everyone was tired but content. After a quick wash, Arun slipped into bed, his mind unexpectedly drifting back to Riya. Lying there in the stillness of the night, he thought about how lucky he was to have avoided a serious relationship with her. If he had pursued someone as fickle and unpredictable as Riya, who changed her mind like the weather, he would have missed out on the incredible opportunity of having Meera by his side.

"Thank God for saving me," Arun thought, feeling immense gratitude. Meera was different—steadfast, sincere, and someone he could envision spending his life with. He smiled at the thought, relieved to have found someone so genuine. It wasn't long before he fell into a deep, peaceful sleep.

The next morning, everyone woke early to prepare for the day ahead. After a quick breakfast, it was time for Meera's family and Arun to say their goodbyes to his parents and Neha. The farewell was warm and filled with affectionate words. Arun's parents, especially his mother, made Meera's family promise they would visit again soon. Arun signaled discreetly to Neha that he would call her later, to which she gave a knowing smile.

As they began their journey back to the village, the car was quieter than usual. Arun, being the disciplined driver he was, focused on the road. He didn't talk much when driving, especially on long trips. Still, he couldn't help but steal a few glances at Meera through the rearview mirror. Her calm presence brought him a sense of peace, and he smiled inwardly, content with the way things were progressing between them.

To keep the journey light, Arun popped in a cassette with soft music, letting the melodies fill the car. It provided a soothing background to their thoughts as they all enjoyed the quiet drive back home. The music, the tranquility of the early morning, and the anticipation of what the future held created an atmosphere of quiet comfort.

This chapter of their lives, filled with laughter, love, and the promise of something more, was just beginning.

Chapter 18: A Matchmaker's Reward

After a long day at the Police Station, Arun finally found a moment of peace and sat down with a steaming cup of coffee in hand. He pulled out his phone and dialed Neha's number, feeling a mixture of anticipation and curiosity about their conversation. As soon as she picked up, her voice burst through the line, filled with excitement.

"So, how are things, Mr. Silent?" Neha teased, her playful tone instantly lightening Arun's mood. "I've been waiting for your call!"

Arun chuckled softly, taking a sip of his coffee. "Yeah, sorry about that. Things have been hectic at work. But to answer your burning question—yes, I managed to reveal my feelings to Meera."

Neha gasped dramatically. "Oh my gosh, finally! So, how did it go? Spill the details. I need to know everything!"

Arun leaned back, smiling as he replayed the moment in his mind. "I told her yesterday in the library. It was... emotional, to say the least. I said what I've been holding inside for a long time. And she feels the same way, Neha."

Neha let out a little squeal of delight. "I knew it! I knew she had feelings for you too. You should have seen the way she looked at you during dinner—like you were the only one in the room. I'm so happy for you two!"

Arun's heart swelled with happiness, but before he could respond, Neha jumped back in. "By the way, I've been doing some 'matchmaker work' myself," she said with a mischievous grin in her voice. "I casually brought up Meera during lunch yesterday with Mom and Dad."

Arun raised an eyebrow, intrigued. "Oh really? And how did that go?"

Neha couldn't contain her excitement. "It went better than I expected! Dad was all praise, saying Meera is an adorable, charming, and quiet girl. You know how picky he can be, right? And Mom... well, she already seems impressed. She said Meera is not only a good cook but also hardworking, just like Martha."

Arun's grin widened as he listened, feeling a sense of relief. "That's great to hear. But what did they say when you, uh, jokingly suggested she could be their future daughter-in-law?"

Neha giggled. "Oh, you won't believe Dad's response. He laughed and said, 'Who knows? Arun might already be engaged to someone else.' And I just casually threw in, 'Well, if not...' And you know what Dad said?"

Arun's interest peaked. "What?"

Neha paused for dramatic effect. "He said, 'then of course, I'd have no objection. They're a decent, well-known family with little baggage.' And guess what? Mom agreed with him! So... looks like you've got the green light from both of them."

Arun blinked in surprise, his heart racing. He hadn't expected things to go so smoothly with his parents. "Wow, Neha, I don't even know what to say. You've been a miracle worker."

Neha chuckled. "You owe me for this one, big brother! I've paved the way for you. A little token of appreciation wouldn't hurt your personal matchmaker."

Arun laughed, shaking his head. "Don't worry, you'll get your reward. You've definitely earned it."

Neha's voice softened, her teasing tone replaced with sincerity. "I'm really happy for you, Arun. You deserve this. Meera is perfect for you, and I can already see you two building a wonderful life together."

Arun's chest tightened with emotion. "Thanks, Neha. I couldn't have done any of this without you."

"Well, that's what little sisters are for, right? Now, go plan your next move. You've got the hardest part done. Just don't mess it up now!" she teased.

"I'll try my best," Arun replied, grinning from ear to ear.

As the call ended, Arun couldn't help but feel a sense of peace wash over him. Everything was falling into place, thanks to Neha's subtle nudges and his parents' unexpected approval. With his feelings out in the open and both families warming up to the idea, the future was looking brighter than ever.

And now, it was time to make good on his promise—to give Neha the best gift he could think of for helping him in this incredible journey of love.

Chapter 19: A Token of Affection

Arun had been thinking about the necklace ever since he ordered it. After consulting a friend who knew a skilled gold craftsman, he knew this piece was perfect—delicate, genuine, and crafted with care. Without hesitation, he ordered two sets: one for Neha, in gratitude for all her help, and one for Meera, a token of his love.

A couple of weeks later, Arun found time to visit Meera. On Sunday afternoon, he took the jewellery box meant for her and left the quarters, excitement bubbling within him. When he arrived at Meera's house and knocked on the door, she answered almost immediately. Her face lit up with joy at the sight of him.

"Arun! What a surprise!" she exclaimed, stepping aside to let him in.

"I hope I'm not intruding. I should've called first, but I—" he began, but Meera waved her hand with a smile, cutting him off.

"No, no! You're always welcome. Besides, my parents are out at a funeral. They won't be back until later this evening. It's just me."

There was a moment of awkwardness as both of them realized how alone they were. Arun chuckled lightly, scratching the back of his head. "I really should've called. But the funny thing is, I don't even know your phone number," he admitted, his voice lighthearted.

Meera laughed softly, her nerves loosening up. "Neither do I know yours! Can you believe that?"

They both laughed at the absurdity of it, and the tension seemed to dissolve. But in the back of Meera's mind, she was feeling a bit anxious. *How do I keep him entertained? What should I do to make him feel comfortable?* She thought about the lunch she was supposed to make for herself, and an idea struck her.

"Would you like to come into the kitchen with me?" she asked, shyly. "I was about to start making lunch... maybe you could help?"

Arun smiled, a mischievous glint in his eyes. "Sure! But only if you trust me not to ruin the food."

Meera giggled, shaking her head. "I'm sure you'll do just fine. Come on."

They moved into the cozy kitchen together, and the atmosphere was immediately more relaxed. Arun rolled up his sleeves and washed the vegetables while Meera prepared the stove. They talked and laughed like a newly married couple, the casual intimacy of their conversations flowing naturally.

"You know," Arun began, washing a few tomatoes, "I'm not exactly a pro in the kitchen, but I can handle the basics."

Meera raised an eyebrow, amused. "Oh really? And what's the most complicated dish you've ever made?"

Arun thought for a moment, then grinned. "Instant noodles."

Meera burst into laughter, almost dropping the pot she was holding. "Noodles? That doesn't count!"

"Hey!" Arun defended himself, pretending to be hurt. "You try boiling water without burning it. It's harder than it looks."

They both laughed again, their playful banter making the air feel light. The sound of their laughter filled the house as Meera focused on cooking a delicious meal—spiced chicken curry with rice and a side of vegetables. Arun helped where he could, washing ingredients and tasting bits of the sauce, giving exaggerated compliments on how great everything smelled.

After they finished the meal, they sat down to eat, and Arun couldn't stop complimenting her cooking.

"You weren't lying," Arun said between bites, "This is amazing. You're an incredible cook, Meera."

She blushed slightly, looking down at her plate. "Thank you... but it's nothing fancy. Just a simple meal."

Arun reached across the table and gently touched her hand. "It's perfect, just like you."

Her heart skipped a beat at his words. She glanced up at him, and for a moment, they simply looked at each other, the connection between them deepening.

Once the meal was over, Arun reached into his pocket and pulled out the small jewellery box. "I have something for you," he said, sliding it across the table toward her.

Meera looked at him, puzzled. "What's this?"

"Open it," he urged, a soft smile on his face.

She opened the box, and her eyes widened in surprise at the delicate necklace resting inside. "Arun... it's beautiful," she whispered, her voice full of emotion.

"I thought of you when I saw it," he said quietly, watching her reaction. "But if you don't like it, I—"

"Arun," she interrupted gently, closing the box and placing it back on the table. "It's not that I don't like it. It's beautiful... but you didn't need to spend money on me. I don't need gifts. I just need you."

Arun felt his heart swell with emotion at her words. He stood up, walked over to her, and softly took her hand in his. "Meera, I promised myself that I'd do everything to protect and cherish you. I will love you wholeheartedly until the day I die.

Meera's eyes shimmered with unshed tears. She stood up, holding his hand tightly. "Arun... I love you... so much."

There was a quiet moment between them, filled with the kind of love that didn't need more words. Arun gently kissed her forehead, holding her close.

"I'll always keep my promise, Meera. Believe me."

She smiled, her heart full. "I believe you, Arun. I always will."

As they stood there, wrapped in the warmth of their newfound closeness, Arun remembered the small detail they had both missed earlier. He pulled out his phone with a playful grin.

"Now, before I forget again... what's your phone number?"

Meera laughed, pulling out her own phone. "Let's not make that mistake again," she teased, and they quickly exchanged numbers, sealing their connection in more ways than one.

Chapter 20: A Journey Begins

The day of Arun and Meera's wedding arrived, and it was nothing short of magnificent. The grand police ceremony took place at the city's most prestigious venue, an elaborate affair where tradition met honor. Arun, dressed in his immaculate police uniform, stood tall and proud, his presence commanding the attention of everyone present. The gleaming brass buttons on his uniform reflected the sunlight, and his stature exuded both strength and dignity.

Meera, on the other hand, looked ethereal. She walked down the aisle in a stunning ivory maxi, her veil gently flowing behind her like soft clouds. She truly resembled an angel, her beauty radiant and delicate. Her eyes sparkled with joy, and a soft smile played on her lips as she caught sight of Arun waiting for her at the altar.

The guests, composed of high-ranking police officers, family, and friends, could not take their eyes off the couple. Whispers of admiration filled the room.

"Such a perfect match," one of the officers commented quietly to his wife.

"They look like they were made for each other," another guest agreed, nodding in approval.

As Meera reached Arun's side, he couldn't help but gaze at her in awe. His heart swelled with love and pride, and when he took her hand, it felt as if their worlds had finally aligned. The ceremony proceeded with all the grandeur one could expect for a distinguished officer and his bride. As vows were exchanged, there wasn't a dry eye in the room.

After the ceremony, the newlyweds were congratulated by a sea of guests. The higher ranks of the police force shook Arun's hand, offering their heartfelt congratulations. "You've done well, Arun," his commanding officer said with a smile. "And your wife is as lovely as they come."

Amid the celebrations, Neha beamed with joy for her brother. After the formalities, Arun slipped away for a moment and handed Neha the jewelry box he had brought for her. "This is for you," he said, smiling warmly. "A small token of my appreciation for everything you've done."

Neha's eyes widened when she opened the box, revealing the delicate necklace. "Arun... this is beautiful," she whispered, touched by the gesture. "But you didn't have to—"

"I did," Arun interrupted gently. "You've been my rock through all of this. You deserve something special."

She hugged him tightly, her voice full of emotion. "Thank you, Arun. I'm so happy for you."

After the ceremony and the grand reception that followed, Arun and Meera changed into their travel clothes. Arun's uniform was replaced by a crisp suit, while Meera donned a simple yet elegant dress. Together, hand in hand, they made their way to the airport, ready to begin the next chapter of their lives.

As they stepped outside, the warmth of the afternoon sun greeted them, but the warmth in Meera's heart was mixed with a bittersweet feeling. Her parents stood by their car, visibly emotional. Meera's mother had tears glistening in her eyes, a blend of pride and sadness reflected in her expression. "You'll always be our little girl," she said, pulling Meera into a tight embrace. "No matter where you go, remember that we'll always be here for you."

Meera's father, though trying to maintain a strong demeanor, couldn't hide the tremor in his voice as he spoke. "You've made us proud, Meera. Just promise us you'll take care of each other and come back with wonderful stories."

Meera nodded, her heart aching at the thought of leaving her parents behind for two weeks. "I will, Dad. We'll make sure to stay in touch," she said, her voice thick with emotion.

Meanwhile, Arun's parents stood nearby, their faces radiant with joy and love. His mother stepped forward, her eyes sparkling with tears of happiness. "Meera, you are now part of our family," she said, embracing her warmly. "May your life together be filled with love and laughter. You have a wonderful heart, and I know you will bring so much happiness to Arun."

Arun's father, a proud smile on his face, added, "Together, you will create a beautiful life. Support each other, and always communicate openly. Remember, love is the foundation of a happy marriage."

Arun stepped forward, gratitude shining in his eyes. "Thank you, Mom and Dad. Your support means the world to us. We promise to cherish and uphold the values you've taught us."

As they pulled away from the curb, Meera turned back one last time to see her parents and Arun's parents waving, their smiles masking the sadness of watching their children embark on this new adventure. In that moment, Meera felt a surge of love for both families and knew that this was not just a departure but a transition into a new life—one that would always be rooted in the love and values they had instilled in her.

With Arun's hand securely in hers, Meera took a deep breath, allowing the excitement of their honeymoon to wash over her, even as her heart held a tender ache for their parents.

"Singapore awaits us," Arun said with a grin, and Meera smiled back, ready to embrace the adventures that lay ahead.

As the plane took off, leaving behind the familiar city skyline, Meera looked at Arun and smiled. "Can you believe it? We're finally married," she whispered, her voice soft with disbelief.

Arun squeezed her hand gently. "It feels like a dream, but it's real," he replied, looking at her with adoration. "And we're just getting started."

The flight to Singapore was filled with soft conversations, stolen glances, and quiet moments of reflection. They were both excited, not just for the honeymoon but for the life they were about to build together.

When they finally landed in Singapore, the air was warm and fragrant with the scent of tropical flowers. As they entered their luxurious hotel suite, Arun could no longer hold back his feelings. He pulled Meera close and kissed her—softly at first, then deeper, more passionately, as though he wanted to pour all his love into that one moment. It was a kiss that spoke of promises, dreams, and a future they would share.

Meera's heart raced as she wrapped her arms around him, melting into the warmth and security of his embrace. When they finally broke apart, they were both breathless, their foreheads resting against each other.

"I love you, Arun," Meera whispered, her voice filled with emotion.

"And I love you," Arun replied, his eyes never leaving hers. "More than you can imagine."

The rest of their honeymoon was nothing short of magical. They explored the vibrant streets of Singapore, enjoyed candlelit dinners by the bay, and strolled through lush gardens hand in hand. Every moment felt like a fairytale, and each day was filled with laughter, love, and the kind of happiness they had both longed for.

As the sun set on their final evening, they sat together on the balcony of their hotel room, watching the city lights twinkle in the distance. The world was at their feet, and their hearts were full.

"Here's to the beginning of our forever," Arun said softly, raising a glass of wine.

Meera smiled, clinking her glass against his. "And to everything that comes with it."

In that moment, they knew that no matter what life had in store for them, they would face it together—stronger, braver, and more in love than ever before.